Beauty and the Beast

❧ Fairy Tale Treasury ❧

Adapted by
Jane Jerrard

Illustrations by
Burgandy Nilles

Publications International, Ltd.

There once was a rich man who fell upon hard times. When the ships that carried his fortune were lost at sea, he and his children had to move to the country. There they lived very plainly. While his older children were unhappy with their new life, his youngest daughter, Beauty, tried to make the best of things.

One day, the man heard that one of his ships had sailed safely into harbor. He decided to go and see for himself.

His other children asked their father to bring them back expensive presents. But Beauty asked only for a single rose.

Once he arrived in town, Beauty's father discovered that the good news about his ship was not true. While returning home through a thick forest, the unlucky man was lost in a terrible snowstorm. Suddenly, up ahead, he saw flowering trees!

The man had discovered an enchanted castle. Though no one was around, he found a cozy room with a tray of food set out for him. He ate hungrily, then fell asleep.

The next day, the man remembered Beauty's request, so he picked a rose for her. Suddenly, an ugly Beast appeared! The Beast was very angry that the man was stealing from him. Beauty's father explained that the rose was for his daughter.

The Beast said he would not kill the man if Beauty would come to stay with him. He promised to treat her kindly. The poor man returned home and told his family about his promise. The next day, Beauty went bravely with her father.

When she met the Beast, Beauty was very frightened by his terrible face, but he spoke to her gently. He asked if she would stay with him to save her father's life.

Beauty agreed to stay. So she made the Beast's castle her home. She had her own big room, and spent her days alone, exploring the wonders of the enchanted castle.

Every night, she sat down to dinner with the Beast. He was quite fierce-looking, but his voice was quiet and gentle, and he always spoke kindly to Beauty. Soon, she was no longer afraid of him and even found herself growing fond of him.

After dinner, they would walk through the beautiful gardens and talk. No matter what they spoke of, the Beast asked Beauty the same question every night:

"Am I very ugly?" he asked. She answered that he was, but that she liked him anyway.

"Then will you marry me, Beauty?" he would say, and she would beg him not to ask her that.

Beauty was happy in the magical castle, and she had grown very fond of the Beast. But she never stopped missing her brothers and sisters and her loving father.

One night she asked the Beast to let her go home for a visit. He made her promise to come back in two months and gave her a ring with a large jewel in it. He explained that if she turned it on her finger, she would be home the next day!

The next morning, Beauty awoke to her father's voice. She was in her own bed! Her family was very happy to see her. Her father's luck had returned, and they were rich once more.

As time passed, Beauty missed her happy days in the castle. She especially missed the Beast and their evening talks. She grew restless, but she was afraid to tell her family that she wanted to leave.

One evening, Beauty looked into the ring and saw the Beast. He was dying! Beauty turned the ring on her finger and was suddenly with him.

"Oh, please don't die, gentle Beast!" cried Beauty. "I love you!"

At her words, the Beast leaped up. He was changed into a handsome prince! Beauty's love had freed him from an evil spell. So Beauty and her Prince were married, and they lived happily in the enchanted castle.